Anonymous

As to Kearsarge Mountain

and the corvette named for it

Anonymous

As to Kearsarge Mountain
and the corvette named for it

ISBN/EAN: 9783337288426

Printed in Europe, USA, Canada, Australia, Japan

Cover: Foto ©Andreas Hilbeck / pixelio.de

More available books at **www.hansebooks.com**

KEARSARGE MOUNTAIN,

AND THE

CORVETTE

NAMED FOR IT.

" Kearsarge,
Lifting his Titan forehead to the sun."—WHITTIER.

CONCORD, N. H.:
PRINTED BY THE REPUBLICAN PRESS ASSOCIATION.
1879.

THE MOUNTAIN.

KEARSARGE mountain is in Merrimack county, New Hampshire, within the towns of Andover, New London, Salisbury, Sutton, Warner, and Wilmot. Its height, as given in Prof. Hitchcock's Geology of New Hampshire, is 2,943 feet above tide-water. It is a massive, lonely peak, standing in stately grandeur, hard by busy towns and great lines of railway. The view from its summit is extended and picturesque, as may be imagined, by those who have had no opportunity of personal observation, from the following careful list of prominent peaks to be seen from its summit : In Hillsborough county, Pack Monadnock (2,288 feet in height), Crotched (2,066) ; in Cheshire county, Grand Monadnock (3,186), Pitcher (2,170) ; (Wachusett, near Worcester, Mass., can be seen in the clearest days) ; in Sullivan county, Croydon (2,789), Melvin (2,134), Lovell's (2,487) ; in Merrimack county, Sunapee (2,638), Ragged (2,256), Stewart's (1,808), McCoy's (1,590) ; in Grafton county, Moose (2,326), Prospect (2,072), Stinson (2,707),

Cuba (2,927), Cardigan (3,156), Whiteface (4,007), Tri-pyramid (4,150), Passaconaway (4,200), Osceola (4,397), Sandwich Dome (3,999), Carrigan (4,678), Lincoln (5,101), Lafayette (5,259), Cannon (3,850), Twins (5,000), and Moosilauke (4,811). The Franconia Notch can be distinctly traced.

In Vermont, Ascutney (3,186) is visible, and all the Green Mountain range, as far south as the vicinity of Rutland; Joy Peak, the finest outlined mountain in Vermont, near the Canada line, west of Newport; Mt. Mansfield (4,360), Camel's Hump (4,188), and Killington Peak (3,675), near Rutland. These are the chief heights.

In Coös county, Washington, Adams, and Jefferson are easily distinguished. Nearly all the prin cipal peaks west of the Saco and south of the Ammonoosuc rivers are visible ; and, beside the Mount Washington range, may be seen, in Carroll county, Doublehead (3,120), Pequawket (3,251), Chocorua (3,540), Ossipee (2,361), Red Hill (2,033), Cropple Crown (2,100), Mote (3,200), and others.

Portions of Winnipiseogee, Sunapee, and Newfound lakes, besides fifteen or twenty ponds, and eighteen villages or cities, are within sight, while the course of Merrimack river can be traced as far south as Hooksett.

Kearsarge is not like a beggar, either in history or in lighter literature. Its rugged yet graceful outlines are associated with the witchery of the Indian legend, the story of the hunters' camp, and the prosaic pages of colonial chronicle. When Passaconaway, the great sachem of the Merrimack valley, summoned his friends and liegemen to the wedding of his daughter, as Whittier relates in the " Bridal of Penacook," they brought to the nuptial feast,—

> " Steaks of the brown bear, fat and large,
> From the rocky slopes of the Kearsarge."

It appears that there were in New England few better dwelling-places for the Indian than this region. There were fish for his net and spear, game for his snare and arrow, and meadows for the rude culture of maize ; and these, also, were the attractions which brought hither the white frontiersman to push away with axe and plow the red owners of the soil.

During the dread years of French and Indian warfare against New England settlers. a full share of death and captivity was brought to the people around Kearsarge. The old mountain saw the smoke of the lodges of those dusky warriors who had the temerity to attempt to carry Hannah Duston, the wife of a frontier clergyman, into northern captivity, as well as that of which Daniel Webster said, " when it curled over the frozen hills, there was no similar evidence of a white man's habitation between it and the settlements on the rivers of Canada."

Then came the Revolutionary war, and within its sight Ebenezer Webster and Gordon Hutchins and John Stark mustered the men who marched to Bennington, and made the victory at Saratoga possible.

In still later years; along the ancient neighboring highways, poured the traffic of northern New Hampshire, Vermont, and Canada. To crop the sweet grasses of the mountain pastures, the cattle of Newbury, Amesbury, and other Massachusetts towns were annually driven. And here again the captivating pen of the loved poet of New England finds inspiration. In "The Drovers" he says,—

*　　*　　*　　*　　*　　*

"Day after day our way has been
　O'er many a hill and hollow;
By lake and stream, by wood and glen,
　Our stately drove we follow;
Through dust-clouds, rising thick and dun,
　As smoke of battle o'er us,
Their white horns glisten in the sun,
　Like plumes and crests before us.

"We see them slowly climb the hill,
　As slow behind it sinking;
Or thronging close, from road-side rill,
　Or sunny lakelet, drinking:
Now crowding in the narrow road
　In thick and struggling masses,
They glare upon the teamster's load,
　Or rattling coach that passes.

*　　*　　*　　*　　*　　*

" The night is falling, comrades mine!
Our footsore beasts are weary,
And through yon elms the tavern sign
Looks out upon us cheery:
To-morrow, eastward with our charge
We'll go to meet the dawning,
Ere yet the pines of Kearsarge
Have seen the sun of morning."

The region could spare much that belongs to it in story, and still much would remain; but the people who dwell around the mountain have observed for four years a persistent attempt to filch its name and historic renown, and have kept silence as long as silence is proper. This attempt at historical theft is stated, in the language of its would-be perpetrator, in Johnson's Cyclopædia, in the following words:

" Kearsarge Mount, a conspicuous mountain in Carroll Co., N. H. On the suggestion of the wife of the Assistant Secretary of the Navy, a daughter of Levi Woodbury, of New Hampshire, the Secretary, in 1861, named the vessel which sunk the Alabama in 1864 after this mountain. Another one of the same name in Merrimack Co, N. H., formerly called Kya-Sarga, has been erroneously claimed for this honor.

G. V. FOX."

This attempt to garble minor history is said to have its origin in two purposes,—one, to gratify a personal pique at Admiral Winslow, who will be hereafter mentioned; and the other, to endeavor to connect the family of Levi Woodbury with the expression of just one sentiment akin to loyalty during the years of the Rebellion. Whatever the purpose, it has been followed with audacity and perseverance, and time and money have been expended in its behalf. It is therefore expedient to set forth in opposition thereto the following collection of facts and opinions, incomplete though it be.

At the outset the compiler may be permitted to say, that neither Secretary Welles nor Mr. Fox, formerly of the Navy Department, ever lost any personal fame, however petty, by reason of not claiming it. For example, Mr. Welles, in the letter referred to on page 24, says,—

"At the commencement of our civil war, when we were building a number of vessels, it seemed a favorable opportunity to give our naval vessels *American* names, instead of imitating the English, and copying from their Naval Register."

This is a claim, by implication, that, prior to the war and his secretaryship, our naval vessels had no American names. The truth is, that in the Naval Register for 1860 are, among others, the following: Ohio, Delaware, Alabama, Potomac, Saratoga, Niagara, Roanoke, Colorado, Merrimack, Minnesota, Susquehanna, Powhatan, Saranac, Iroquois, Wyandotte, Dacotah, and Pocahontas; and, in fact, more than half the names of vessels then in the navy were of distinctive American origin. The busiest vessel at the outbreak of the Rebellion was the Pawnee.

Mr. Welles, in the letter above referred to, dated Sept. 27, 1875, recites the pretensions of Mr. Fox in regard to the name of the corvette Kearsarge, and half favors them ; but he says, with obvious truthfulness, " *although after the lapse of fourteen years I may not recollect them.*" He wrote to like purport in this respect at other times, but it is apparent that he did so at the solicitation of Mr. Fox, and that he depended upon the presumed knowledge and memory of the latter person, who, on or about Sept. 17, 1875, paid the venerable ex-secretary a visit, for the purpose of coloring his recollections on this subject. It is, therefore, fair to say, that this "old sailor's yarn" in behalf of the Carroll county mountain rests on the testimony of Mr. Fox alone ; and it can be determined how much reliance to place on his memory—if, indeed, it be a matter of memory—in affairs of this nature, when it is known that in some studied remarks to the city council of Boston, Jan. 18, 1875, in an unsuccessful attempt to attach the name of Farragut to a public square, he declared the name of the great Admiral to have been Loyal Farragut, when all the world, except himself, knows it to have been David Glascoe Farragut, and that Loyal Farragut is a son of the Admiral.

Mr. Fox's stories seem to be of that kind usually told to the marines.

Let us glance at history and topography for some mention of Kearsarge mountain.

On Gardner's map of a survey of Merrimack river, ordered by the General Court of Massachusetts in 1638, and made by Nathaniel Woodward in the spring of 1639,* only nineteen years after the landing of the pilgrims, Kearsarge is shown in its correct position, and is called Carasaga. The original of this map, attested by John Gardner's autograph, was discovered in 1876, in the archives of the Essex (Mass.) County Commissioners, by Geo. E. Emery, Esq., of Lynn. It has since been photographed. In Woodward's surveying party were two Natick Indians, and Carasarga is thought to mean, in the dialect of that race, *Notch-pointed Mountain of Pines*. This is believed to be the meaning of the name in its successive forms, the differences springing from different Indian dialects. Until 1798 Kearsarge was covered with a dense growth of pine and spruce, but in August of that year a great fire swept over the mountain, the summit of which has a notched appearance from points in the upper Merrimack valley, and as far north as East Andover. Woodward's surveying party appear to have ascended Kearsarge, because

---

* Some authorities say this map was made in 1652.

Lake Winnipiseogee is shown on the map as it appears from the summit of that mountain.

"In a journal of a scouting party, commanded by Samuel Willard, of Lancaster, Mass., in July, 1725, the mountain was seen and spoken of as 'Cu-sà-gee.'

"On a map of New Hampshire, by Joseph Blanchard and Samuel Langdon—afterward President of Harvard college—published in 1761, the same mountain is called 'Kya-sa-ge,' and *no name* given to the mountain in Carroll county.

"On a map of a survey made by Samuel Holland, Esq., the King's surveyor of Northern New Hampshire, 1773-4, and published 1784, the same mountain is accurately laid down and called 'Kyar Sarga,—by Indians, Cowissewaschook.' On this map the mountain in Carroll county is distinctly marked, but *no name* given to it.

"In June, 1793, the legislature of New Hampshire passed an 'act to set off sundry lots of land from a place called Kear Sarge Gore, in the county of Hillsborough (since within Merrimack county), and to annex the same, with the inhabitants thereon, to New London, in said county.' This act conclusively proves that the said mountain was recognized and publicly known at that time by the name of Kearsarge.

"On all maps, geographical surveys, histories, and registers of New Hampshire since that time, the said mountain has been described or referred to, invariably, as in the same locality, bearing the same name, the variations in spelling being of no account."

Rev. Dr. Bouton, the State Historian, in a communication to the Concord (N. H.) *Statesman*, of Aug. 3, 1876, recites most of the above facts (the quoted words being his own), decides that the true name of the Carroll county mountain is Pigwacket, and concludes as follows:

"On the settlement of the Pigwacket country, by people from towns in the immediate vicinity of the true, old, and venerable mountain in Merrimack county, by a natural law of association they transferred and appropriated the name, which they held in honor, to the most conspicuous one of the hills in the region of their new residence. Rising before them in grandeur and beauty, somewhat like their own 'peerless' Kearsarge, they gave to this eminence the same cherished name.* Hence, when Dr. Belknap published his history of New Hampshire, with his new map, he gave it the *local* name which the people living there had begun to call it. By so lending his authority to a local partiality, he confused both our geography and history; for, on the same map in which he introduced this new name to one of the 'Pigwacket' hills, he had already marked, in its proper locality and with its time-honored name, the true and only Kearsarge of New Hampshire. Hence it was both proper and important that Mr. Carrigain, in his new map,

---

* Singularly enough, the name of Kearsarge has been carried to California, and given to two peaks in that state,—one, not far from the Nevada line where it crosses the 36th parallel; the other, near the town of Independence.

published by authority of the legislature, should give
the mountain in Carroll county its just and appropriate name, Pigwacket,—a name, I may add, of
great historic significance and honor. It commem-
orates the fact that that section of country was
once the head-quarters of a powerful Indian tribe,
and still more, the 'great fight' in 1725, in which
the heroic and honored Capt. Lovewell fell, as did
also Paugus, the bold Sagamore of the Pequakett
tribe. That 'fight' opened that fertile country to
a prosperous civilization.

"We need only add, that the rightful claim of
the name Kearsarge to the mountain in Merrimack
county being established by priority of unbroken
usage for more than three-score years, other ques-
tions incidental thereto may easily be settled. The
honor of the name, for example, given to our vic-
torious ship of war, the Kearsarge, that sunk the
Alabama, even though claimed by mistake for the
mountain in Carroll county, would seem rightfully
to belong to the ancient and only true mountain of
that name in New Hampshire. So, also, should it
be deemed wise and expedient to clear our mountain geography of duplicate names so as to accord
with the records of history, it would be most suitable to restore to that conspicuous eminence the
name given it on Carrigain's map,—alike honora-
ble to the ancient name and to the heroic deeds
for which that section of the country will ever be
celebrated."

The Committee on Towns and Parishes of the
New Hampshire Legislature had the subject under
consideration in 1876, and reported as follows:

"From the evidence submitted, it appears that there are two mountains in New Hampshire now known by the name of Kearsarge,—one in Merrimack, and the other in Carroll county,—and the orthography of the word, like that of others derived from the Indians, has undergone various changes. On the elaborate English map by Blanchard and Langdon, from surveys made in 1761, and published in 1768, the name Kyasage is given to the mountain in Merrimack county. The Holland map of 1784 gives the name of Kyar-Sarga to the mountain in Merrimack county, and no name to that in Carroll county; and your committee are unanimously of the opinion that the mountain in Merrimack county is justly entitled to the name of Kearsarge.

GEO. C. GILMORE,
For the Committee."

In regard to the Carroll county mountain, Dr. Bouton says:

"It should be understood that the entire section of country where that mountain is located, has, from its first discovery by white men, been known and called by the name of the Pigwacket country: so called from a tribe of Indians, Pequaketts, that lived on the rich meadows along the Saco river, having the adjacent hill country for huntinggrounds. It was so called in 1642, when the first visit was made by Darby Field, and soon after by others, to the White Hills. In the Pigwacket country the great fight took place, May, 1725, between the company commanded by Capt. John Lovewell

and the Pequakett Indians under Paugus. In
every period since, at least till within a few years,
in historical and geographical accounts of that
country, including Fryeburg, Brownfield, Conway,
and Chatham, the region has always been spoken
of under the same name. Accordingly we find,—

" 1. That in the journal of Capt. Samuel Willard, before referred to, he says he saw ' Pigwack-
ett' in a north-eastern direction from the Grand
Monadnock.*

" 2. In 1741, Walter Bryant, Esq., surveyed the
eastern line of New Hampshire, and went as far
as ' Pigwaket,' where he saw ' the Pigwaket plain
or intervale land, as also Pigwaket river.'

" 3. On a map by Mitchell and Hazzen, survey-
ors of New Hampshire, 1750, the ' Pigwakket
hills' are laid down in a group in the north part of
the Pigwacket country.

" 4. Settlements were commenced in that region
about 1765–1770. When a grant was made of the
township of Conway, Sept. 30, 1765, of six miles
square, it was described as ' at a place called Pigwacket.' The settlements at Conway, Chatham,
and Fryeburg were made chiefly by emigrants from
Concord, Boscawen, Salisbury, and Andover—
persons who had always lived in sight and under
the shadow of the Kearsarge mountain in Merrimack county.

" 5. In a memorial of committees of inhabitants
of Conway, Fryeburg, and Brownfield, dated July

---

* The Appalachian Mountain Club has demonstrated the
possibility of this by two unsuccessful attempts, said to
have been made at the expense of Mr. Fox, to prove the
contrary.

8, 1776, presented to the General Court of New Hampshire, asking for aid and protection against the Indians, they say,—' The said new plantations consist of about one hundred and thirty families, situated at a place called Pigwacket, upon Saco river.'

" 6. Several years after the settlement of Conway and Fryeburg was begun, the Rev. Timothy Walker, of Concord, made an annual visit thither, to preach and administer ordinances to families of his former charge, and always in his journal called the region Pigwacket."

In a letter dated Sept. 25, 1875, Dr. Bouton says,—

" The true and only mountain in New Hampshire which can rightfully claim the name of Kearsarge, is that in our county of Merrimack."

The *Atlantic Monthly*, for July, 1878, says,—

" The Conway Kearsarge, so often sung by Boston bards and climbed by Boston boots, was really christened after the Merrimack county Kearsarge, both morally and chronologically. The towns adjoining and including the southern mountain (which is situated almost exactly in the geographical centre of New Hampshire),—Warner, Boscawen, Andover, and New London,—were nearly all settled in the earlier half of the last century, while the Conway tract was first occupied late in the seventeen hundreds by emigrants from the Merrimack county region. They must have named the northern

mountain for the southern one, on account of a re-
semblance of outline, which is remote enough from
some points of view, but rather striking from
others."

Citations similar to the foregoing might be mul-
tiplied, and maps, gazetteers, and other works
quoted, but it is believed that if the careful research of a painstaking historian can settle anything, the quotations from Dr. Bouton are sufficient to establish the fact that the mountain in Merrimack county is the noted Kearsarge.

As to the name of the corvette, a little research
has discovered the following

CONTEMPORARY NEWSPAPER MENTION.

Dispatches from Washington give the names of
the new sloops of war—the Kearsarge, Ossipee,
Housatonic, Wachusett, Adirondack, Juniata, and
Tuscarora. Kearsarge is a well known mountain
in Merrimack county, New Hampshire, about
twenty miles north-west of Concord. There is
another mountain north of Lake Winnipiseogee
which modern tourists have confounded with the
true one.—*Boston Journal, June* 4, 1861.

Of the new sloops of war built at Portsmouth,
one will be named Ossipee, and the other Kearsarge. These are Indian words, but, unlike many
of that dialect, pass easily over the tongue. Kearsarge was suggested to the naval department by

2

one of the publishers of this paper. He wrote that, as the Merrimack was burned at Norfolk, it would be gratifying to New Hampshire folks to be again remembered in this matter of names of national vessels, and, in presenting Kearsarge, said it was an isolated and imposing eminence in the centre of the state, in the midst of a loyal people, and that young Ladd, who fell at Baltimore, crying "All hail to the stars and stripes," was buried almost within its shadow, at Alexandria.—*Asa McFarland, in New Hampshire Statesman, June 8, 1861.*

Kearsarge mountain, from which Capt. Winslow's vessel receives its immortal name, is the highest mountain in the county of Merrimack, New Hampshire. Its summit is a mass of granite, presenting an irregular and broken surface. The prospect from the mountain is very wide and beautiful.—*Army and Navy Journal, 1864.*

It was a happy inspiration that gave the name of Kearsarge to one of the most beautiful and fortunate of our ships of war. The appropriateness of the name was from the first apparent to those who, like the writer, have been familiar with the old mountain from earliest recollection. It is, as lately stated, situated very near the centre of the old Granite state, and stands there high above the many surrounding hills, in a country where all is hill and valley, for all the world as if it were the great heart of that hard old state. It is in the towns of Salisbury, Sutton, Andover, Wilmot, New London, and Warner. The mountain is great as well as hard. It is rich in association, tradition, and story, and rich, above all, in the character of the population which lives and grows about and upon the sides of this, to me, the most beautiful of all the mountains of my native state. Like the land they inhabit, though kind, honest, generous, even patriotic, they are in one sense very hard they are a race not easily conquered. I know them well, and know this is true. And when Kearsarge was first announced as the name of the new ship, it seemed like an appropriate recognition of and compliment to this last quality of its hardy sons.—*New York Evening Post, July* 14, 1864.

The sinking of the Alabama by the Kearsarge has given great joy to the soldiers. They are as much gratified as if they had won a victory. The men of the Kearsarge were mainly from New Hampshire. Their ship was built there, and bears the name of the grand old mountain beneath the shadow of which Daniel Webster passed his childhood. The name was selected for the ship by one of the publishers of the *New Hampshire Statesman.* The tourist passing through the Granite state will look with increased pleasure upon the mountain, whose name, bestowed upon a national vessel, will be prominent in the history of the nation.—*Petersburg (Va.) correspondence to Boston Journal, July* 16, 1864.

The purport of the following letter was printed in the Boston *Transcript,* of June 24, 1878. Some sentences omitted then have been restored, and others added; but for convenience' sake the original form is preserved:

To the Editor of the Transcript: When you

open this communication you will say, "Fudge! something more about Kearsarge!" You will be right. The topic may be too small rightfully. to provoke so much controversy, but as with all the rivers of ink which have been shed lately on the subject only half the truth is told, and as your correspondent "F.," in his letter published Thursday, has lugged me into the discussion, I will write such facts as are within my knowledge with tolerable brevity, and as impersonally as the narrative will permit. I know how tedious such controversies are to the general reader, and have never heretofore written a word on this subject for publication ; therefore it cannot be said that I have been a common brawler in the dispute.

Having had from boyhood a high degree of admiration for the Kearsarge of Merrimack county, I often wondered why its name had not been given to some ship. When the war of the Rebellion broke out, with a consequent increase of the navy, it appeared that a fit time had come. On May 31, or June 1, 1861, I wrote a letter to the assistant secretary of the navy (G. V. Fox), suggesting that one of the sloops of war then ordered to be built at Portsmouth be called *Kearsarge*. This letter stated the location of the mountain distinctly (near the centre of the state) ; that it was a bold, isolated eminence ; that its euphonious name had never been given to a ship ; that the soldier of the 6th Massachusetts regiment, who was reported to have exclaimed with his dying breath, as he fell in Baltimore, "*All hail to the stars and stripes!*" was then buried in its shadow ;* that the adoption of

---

* This incident was commemorated in verse by Geo.

the name would gratify the loyal people of the vicinity, who regretted that the frigate Merrimack had fallen into rebel hands ; and closed by asking the assistant secretary, if the suggestion met with his own favor, to bring it to the notice of the secretary. The assistant secretary once stated to me that he remembered receiving and carrying to his residence that letter. It is not now, if it ever was, in the files of the department. It would probably have been more suitable, and the event has proved that it would have been wiser, to have addressed the letter to the secretary of the navy himself. It was written at the office of the *New Hampshire Statesman*, a publication in which I was then concerned, and is said to be now " stowed away among papers in Lowell, Mass.," from which retirement there is probably no reason to hope that it will be called.

It will be noticed that the foregoing statement in regard to the mountain would not apply in any respect to the Pequawket-Kiarsarge of Carroll county.

If anything more had been needed to establish the propriety of offering the name, it might have been found in the fact that on a little territory near the foot of the eastern slope of Kearsarge, Daniel

---

T. Bourne, of New York. The soldier, Luther C. Ladd, was first buried at Alexandria, his birthplace, afterward at Lowell, where the commonwealth of Massachusetts and the city of Lowell dedicated a handsome monument to the memory of his dead comrade and himself. It was of these men that Gov. Andrew telegraphed to the mayor of Baltimore,— " I pray you to cause the bodies of our Massachusetts soldiers, dead in Baltimore, to be immediately laid out, preserved in ice, and tenderly sent to me. All expenses will be paid by this commonwealth."

Webster, John A. Dix, and William Pitt Fessenden were born.

The Kearsarge happened to become famous by sinking the Alabama long ago (on June 19, 1864). After that event a large hotel was built on the side of the Merrimack county mountain, and named, in honor of the ship's captain, the " Winslow House." That hotel was destroyed by fire in 1867, and rebuilt on a larger plan. Admiral Winslow was given a reception in the first house, and was present at the opening of the second (Aug. 12, 1868), when he gave the owner a stand of colors and a picture of the battle. Notable people were there on those occasions, such as the governor of the state, the ex-solicitor of the navy department and assistant secretary of the U. S. treasury, the sergeant-at-arms of the U. S. house of representatives, Paymaster J. A. Smith of the Kearsarge, our ex-minister to Switzerland, army officers, and prominent citizens, who took part in the festivities and addresses of congratulation.

These things were not done in a corner : they were published far and wide, and, so far as I know, no one challenged the existing general belief that the corvette was named for that mountain. In process of time Admiral Winslow died, and a boulder was taken from the side of that Kearsarge to serve as his monument :—but just here the controversy as to the origin of the ship's name was begun, and, as part of the scheme, an attempt was made to worry the family of the admiral into disuse of the boulder. This impertinence failed of its purpose, and the boulder stands on Orange path, Forest Hill Cemetery, Boston, supporting a bronze tablet with the following inscription :

Rear Admiral
JOHN ANCRUM WINSLOW,
U. S. Navy,
Born in Wilmington, N. C.,
Nov. 19, 1811,
Died in Boston, Mass.,
Sept. 29, 1873.
He conducted the memorable
Sea fight in command of
U. S. S. Kearsarge,
When she sunk the Alabama in the
English Channel, June 19, 1864.

———

This boulder from
Kearsarge Mountain, Merrimack county, N. H.,
Is the gift
Of citizens of Warner, N. H., and is erected
to his memory by his wife and
surviving children.

I never heard of any dispute about the origin of
the corvette's name until July, 1875, fourteen years
after she was built, and eleven years after she sunk
the Alabama, when I received a note from your
correspondent " F.," asking me to inform him
about the naming of the Kearsarge ; and I stated to
him the facts narrated in the second paragraph of
this letter. He replied that I was in error in sup-
posing my letter furnished the earliest suggestion
of the name ; that it had been proposed verbally by
a member of his own family ; that he did not at
that time know there were two mountains in New
Hampshire bearing names so nearly alike ; and
that he did not ascertain this fact until after the
sinking of the Alabama, when he obtained the information from Senator James W. Grimes, of Iowa,
a native of New Hampshire.

(It is to be hoped he may never know that there
are two Monadnocks in New England, or that the
rivers Soucook and Suncook both flow in the town
of Pembroke, N. H.)

A letter from J. C. Howell, acting secretary of
the navy, Sept. 28, 1875, says,—"The files and
records of the department have been examined, but
the department is unable to inform you how the
name came to be selected." This is quoted here,
because it is impossible to say what future altera-
tions a ruthless hand, disposed to distort historical
facts, may not be able to effect in the records of the
department.

The name which the records of the navy show
to have been first given to the corvette was " Kearsage," omitting the final "r;" but a few days later,
on June 15, 1861, the correct name of " Kearsarge"
was applied to her. Secretary Welles, in a letter
which is before me, dated Sept. 27, 1875, says he
thought *Kearsage* was right, but that Secretary
Chase corrected his orthography and pronunciation, and after a dispute convinced him that Kearsarge was right. Mr. Welles's exact language is
as follows:

" I first directed that the corvette should be
called Kearsage; but Mr. Chase, a New Hampshire man, corrected my pronunciation and orthography. We had, I recollect. a little dispute, and
that I quoted Gov. Hill, but Mr. Chase convinced
me he was correct."

The corvette appears to me to have been named
when she received the precise designation which
she defiantly carried through storm and battle. It

will be well to remember here that Mr. Chase was
a native of Cornish, a New Hampshire town
which has the Kearsarge of Merrimack county in
view.

Mr. Welles says, "I quoted Gov. Hill." This is
further good evidence that it was the mountain in
Merrimack county for which he named the corvette, Gov. Hill having been a citizen of Concord,
a large land-owner on the side of that mountain,
and enthusiastic with word and pen in regard to it.
In the *Farmers' Monthly Visitor*, conducted by
Isaac Hill, Vol. 1, No. 5, printed at Concord, May
15, 1839, is a two-page description of Kearsarge,
from his own pen, illustrated with a view of the
mountain from Putney's hill in Hopkinton,—a no-
ticeable piece of enterprise for those times. He
wrote the name as Kearsarge, and not as Mr.
Welles understood it.

It is also a fact, that at the time the corvette
was named the Carroll county mountain was generally known as Kiarsarge, a spelling different
from the other. This was the name in common
use at North Conway (although Kiarsarge was
sometimes changed to Pequawket), as I can testify
from personal knowledge, having been a somewhat
frequent visitor to that place before it became a
noted summer resort. That was the name on the
village guideboard. It was the name borne on the
sign of Mr. Thompson's hotel. It was the name
used by the oldest and best informed townspeople.
Residents there have adopted the other spelling
since the naval battle, and since this controversy
began,—a concession which has great significance,
especially since it appears that the change has been
made at the entreaty of your correspondent " F."

Nine tenths of all that has within three years been written on the other side of this subject,—such as communications to newspapers, an article in Johnson's Cyclopædia, essays for club meetings, a pamphlet, correspondence with the coast survey and with historical societies,—has been from the pen of your correspondent " F." So much writing, with references in one series of these productions to those of another, might, in the absence of knowledge of this fact, be mistaken for cumulative testimony. In these contributions to literature, whatever else is said or left unsaid, one is reasonably sure to find it declared of Pequawket-Kiarsarge, with an air of portentous wisdom, that " it looks down on the beautiful valley of North Conway."

It has never seemed to most people, that the point as to whence the suggestion of the name came was of very great public consequence. If it be important to know for which of the mountains the corvette was named, it certainly ought to be considered which mountain bore precisely that name, and had borne it *and no other* almost a century, at the time the corvette was built, and which one Secretary Chase probably had in mind when he, " after a dispute," caused the correct name to be adopted.

The fact is beyond all controversy, that at the date when the corvette was named, the Merrimack county mountain was always called Kearsarge, while the Carroll county mountain was at the same time called, in its immediate vicinity, indifferently Pequawket, or Kiarsarge,*—by careful and studi-

---

* HISTORY OF THE WHITE MOUNTAINS, by Rev. Mr. Willey, a native of the White Mountain region, published

ous persons generally Pequawket, and seldom by anybody called Kearsarge. I presume that in respect to this part of the question the professors of Dartmouth college may be considered as good authority, at least, as any person who did not know, until 1864, that there were two mountains in New Hampshire bearing similar names (and could not spell the name of either correctly)!—and the raised

at North Conway in 1870, p. 205—" Standing upon the summit of Pequawket mountain, one beholds," &c.

Starr King's WHITE HILLS: THEIR LEGENDS, LANDSCAPE, AND POETRY, published in 1860, pp. 12, 14, and 16; also, p. 150—" The true Indian name of·this charming pyramid is Pequawket."

NEW HAMPSHIRE AS IT IS, by E. A. Charlton and Geo. Ticknor, published at Claremont in 1855, p. 469—"Kearsarge mountain is a conspicuous elevation in Warner;" p. 470, " Pequawket mountain is situated in Bartlett."

HARPER'S STATISTICAL GAZETTEER OF THE WORLD, Harper & Bros., New York, 1855—" Kearsarge mountain, Salisbury, Merrimack county, N. H."

PRONOUNCING GAZETTEER OF THE WORLD, J. B. Lippincott & Co., Philadelphia, 1855—" Kearsarge (Keersarj) mountain in Merrimack county, New Hampshire."

[Neither of the last two works makes any mention of Pequawket-Kiarsarge. Either was accessible to the navy and treasury departments when Mr. Welles and Mr. Chase had their dispute.]

DANIEL WEBSTER'S LETTER to R. M. Blatchford, dated at Franklin, May 3, 1846—"West from the river, nine miles off, is the Kearsarge mountain."

THE WHITE MOUNTAIN GUIDE BOOK, Concord, E. C. Eastman, edition of 1872, and all subsequent editions, p. 190—"At Potter Place may be seen, on the left of the

map of the state, prepared under their direction,
now in the state-house at Concord, calls the Merrimack county mountain Kearsarge, and the Carroll
county mountain Pequawket.

Whether the proposal in my original letter to the
assistant secretary met with so much favor as to be
brought to the attention of the secretary of the navy
as that of another person, is a query which pre-
sents itself, but cannot be considered in this communication. My conclusion is, that either with or
without the aid of that letter, either intentionally or
unintentionally, the name of the mountain in Merrimack county was, and ought to have been, given
to the corvette ; and it can never be obliterated.

track, Kearsarge. This is the mountain for which the
steamer was named that was immortalized by the destruc-
tion of the Alabama." On p. 165, speaking of North
Conway—" Mt. Pequawket, or Kiarsarge, is about three
miles from the village."

COLTON'S GENERAL ATLAS OF THE WORLD (editions of
1871, 1877, and 1878, and others). On the map of New
Hampshire, Kearsarge will be found where it belongs,
and the Carroll county mountain is called Pigwacket.

THE GEOLOGY OF NEW HAMPSHIRE, by Prof. C. H.
Hitchcock, State Geologist, with J. H. Huntington and
others, assistants, published by authority of the state, at
Concord, in 1874, in three royal octavo volumes. invariably
calls the Merrimack county mountain Kearsarge, and the
Carroll county mountain Pequawket.

[These are high authorities. Others might be cited to
an indefinite extent, but the writer would not underrate
the intelligence of readers who know that any attempt to
prove that the mountain in Merrimack county was not,
and that the Carroll county mountain was, always known
as Kearsarge, in the year 1861 and contiguous years, has
no color of truth in it.]

It hardly need be said that I am writing in the
belief that your correspondent " F.," and the assistant secretary above alluded to, are one and the
same person.

It is assuredly true that the corvette Kearsarge
was, to a remarkable degree, a New Hampshire
enterprise. She was built by Portsmouth ship-
wrights. New Hampshire oak was in her frame.
At least one third of her crew came from our granite hills. The Piscataqua was the first water on
which she floated. Four of her officers were from
our state. James S. Thornton, her first lieutenant,
who prepared her for battle, stringing chain cable
along her sides to protect her boilers (a device he
learned by service in Farragut's flag-ship at New
Orleans), who trained her gunners so that those of
Her Majesty's ship the Excellent, who served on
the Alabama, were no match for them, was from
Merrimack, and a great grandson of Matthew
Thornton, a signer of the Declaration of Independence ; and it is worth mentioning here, that the
same Matthew Thornton was one of the original
grantees of the town of Wilmot, within which
town Kearsarge mountain partially lies. John M.
Browne, the surgeon, was from some town in Coös
county. Wm. H. Yeaton and Ezra Bartlett, both
of Stratham, were master's mates,—the last named
a great grandson of Josiah Bartlett, another signer
of the Declaration of Independence. Charles H.
Danforth, a son of Mr. Isaac Danforth, formerly of
this city, was a master's mate on board of her, and
fired the first gun of the battle, at least from our
side. The gallant fellow opened a literary as well
as naval combat when he pulled the lanyard of that
cannon. Thornton, Browne, Bartlett, and Dan-

forth, as well as Paymaster Smith, above mentioned, were highly commended for good conduct.
Mark G. Ham, of Portsmouth, carpenter's mate,
was named for promotion.

H. M'F.

CONCORD, N. H., June 21, 1878.

P. S.   The receipt of the letter mentioned in the
second paragraph of the foregoing is established by
the following notes addressed to the writer of this,
the first of which certainly does not give evidence
of having been written by a person in possession of
any accurate information as to the subject in dispute :

BOSTON, July 10, 1875.

DEAR SIR :   Hon. Daniel Barnard, of Franklin,
N. H., informs me that he understands that you
had the honor of naming the sloop-of-war Kearsarge, and it is stated to have been named from
the Kearsarge in Merrimack county.   Please inform as to the above, and oblige

Yours,   G. V. Fox,
Naval Asst. Sec'y during the war.

BOSTON, July 13, 1875.

DEAR SIR :   Referring to our conversation Tues-
day : have you a copy of the letter you addressed
to me at Washington, and the reply?

Yours truly,   G. V. Fox.

BOSTON, July 26, 1875.

DEAR SIR : I have yours of the 16th inst., but
have not yet received a copy of your letter, the
original of which is amongst my papers, I suppose,
but they are stowed away at Lowell.

Very truly,   G. V. Fox.

THE CORVETTE.

The corvette Kearsarge was built at the navy yard near Portsmouth, under the supervision of Naval Constructor Hanscom, and eight months after her keel was laid went to sea (Feb. 5, 1862) in charge of Commander C. W. Pickering. Between the above date and June, 1864, she visited about thirty foreign ports, some of them several times, seeking rebel privateers and blockade runners. Capt. John A. Winslow took command of her at Fayal, April 8, 1863. This officer, under whose control the Kearsarge was destined to become famous, was of the distinguished Massachusetts family bearing that name, but born in North Carolina, where his parents some time resided. He was appointed to the navy through the favor and influence of Daniel Webster, Feb. 1, 1827, and was in constant service until 1842, when, as a lieutenant, he joined the steam-frigate Missouri, which, being one of the first ships of that class in our navy, was sent for exhibition to the principal ports of the United States; also to Havana and

Vera Cruz, and in 1843 to Europe, with Hon. Caleb Cushing, Minister to China. The Missouri was burned at Gibraltar, and Lieut. Winslow was sent home by our Minister to Spain, with intelligence of the disaster, returning to Spain with dispatches from our government. In December, 1845, he sailed for Mexico in the Cumberland, and was engaged in several boat expeditions up the Rio Grande. In the attack on Tobasco he landed with a division of men, and for his gallantry on that occasion was publicly complimented by Commodore Perry, and offered the command of any vessel he might choose out of fourteen captured. He selected the Morris (named for a son of Commodore Morris, who was shot by the side of Winslow, in a boat, on the way to Tobasco), and sailed to join the fleet at Vera Cruz, taking part in the subsequent naval operations of the war with Mexico. He was attached to the frigate St. Lawrence, of the Pacific squadron, from 1851 to 1855, and was on shore duty afterwards until 1861. At the outbreak of the Rebellion, making application for more active service, he was ordered to report to Commodore Foote on the Mississippi river, and was engaged in the formidable task of creating the gunboat flotilla. He took the first division of that flotilla down the river to join Gen. Grant at Cairo, and on his return was assigned to the command of the Benton. While getting this vessel off a shoal, a heavy chain parted under tremendous strain, and he received a wound from a flying link which disabled him for months. He commanded the expedition up the White river for the relief of Gen. Curtis's army ; and in October, 1862, being then a captain, and having asked for more active duty on the Atlantic coast, he was recalled from the West, and in the following December sent to take command of the Kearsarge. Henceforward he was in constant pursuit of Confederate vessels, or cruising on the dangerous coasts of France and England in the stormiest seasons, and harassed with strict observance of their neutrality laws.

While at Dover, on the English coast, June 13, 1864, Capt. Winslow received information that the rebel privateer Alabama was at Cherbourg, for which latter place he sailed. The Kearsarge was off Cherbourg June 14, and the next day it was reported that the Alabama would soon come out and engage : but four days more elapsed before she appeared, having in the meantime been put in fighting trim, the spoil of merchantmen left in a place of safety, and a complement of renowed English gunners received from Her Majesty's practice ship the " Excellent." On Sunday morning, June 19, the commander of the Alabama having requested a French friend to have prayers said for him, as he could not attend church that day, took his ship from her anchorage, and was convoyed by a French frigate to a position three miles off shore. What happened thereafter is concisely told in Capt. Winslow's report to the Secretary of the Navy :

"At twenty minutes after ten the Alabama was descried coming out of the western entrance, accompanied by the Couronne. I had, in an interview with the admiral at Cherbourg, assured him that in the event of an action occurring with the Alabama, the position of the ship should be so far off shore that no question could be advanced about the line of jurisdiction. Accordingly, to perfect this object, and with the further purpose of drawing the Alabama so far off shore that, if disabled, she could not return, I directed the ship's head seaward, and cleared for action, with the battery pivoted to starboard. Having attained a point about seven miles from the shore, the head of the Kearsarge was turned short around, and the ship steered for the Alabama, my purpose being to run her down, or, if circumstances did not warrant that, to close with her.

" Hardly had the Kearsarge come round before the Alabama sheered, presented her starboard battery, and slowed her engines. On approaching her, at long range of about a mile, she opened her full broadside, the shot cutting some of our rigging, and going over and alongside of us. Immediately I ordered more speed, but in two minutes the Alabama had loaded, and fired another broadside, following it with a third, without damaging us except in rigging.

" We had now arrived within about nine hundred yards of her, and I was apprehensive that another broadside—nearly raking as it was—would prove disastrous. Accordingly I ordered the Kearsarge sheered, and opened on the Alabama. The position of the vessels was now broadside and broadside, but it was soon apparent that Capt. Semmes did not seek close action. I became fearful, lest, after some fighting, he would make for the shore. To defeat this I determined to keep full speed on, and with a port helm to run under the stern of the Alabama, and rake her, if he did not prevent it by sheering and keeping his broadside to us. He adopted this mode as a preventive, and as a consequence the Alabama was forced with a full head of steam into a circular track during the engagement.

" The effect of this manœuvre was such that at the last of the action, when the Alabama would have made off, she was near five miles from shore ; had the action continued from the first in parallel lines, with her head in shore, the line of jurisdiction would have been reached. The firing of the Alabama from the first was rapid and wild : toward the close of the action her firing became better. Our men, who had been cautioned against rapid firing without direct aim, were much more deliberate ; and the instructions given to point the heavy guns below rather than above the waterline, and clear the deck with the lighter ones, were fully observed.

" I had endeavored, with a port helm, to close in with the Alabama ; but it was not until just before the close of the action that we were in a position to use grape. This was avoided, however, by her surrender. The effect of the training of our men was evident : nearly every shot from our guns was telling fearfully on the Alabama, and in the seventh rotation on the circular track, she winded, setting

fore trysail and two jibs, with head in shore. Her
speed was now retarded, and by winding, her port
broadside was presented to us with only two guns
bearing, not having been able, as I learned afterward, to shift over but one. I saw now that she
was at our mercy, and a few more well directed
guns brought down her flag. I was unable to ascertain whether it had been hauled down or shot
away, but a white flag having been displayed over
her stern, our fire was reserved. Two minutes had
not more than elapsed before she again opened on
us with the two guns on the port side. This drew
our fire again, and the Kearsarge was immediately
steamed ahead and laid across her bows for raking.
The white flag was still flying, and our fire was
again reserved. Shortly after this her boats were
seen to be lowering, and an officer in one of them
came alongside and informed us the ship had sur-
rendered and was fast sinking. In twenty minutes
from this time the Alabama went down."

Semmes and forty of his men were picked up by
the English yacht Deerhound, and landed in England.

Soon after the battle, English newspapers published accounts of it so false and mistaken, about
damage to the Kearsarge, etc., that Capt. Winslow
addressed a short letter to the London *Daily News*,
contradicting all such "twaddle," saying, "I sup-
posed the action, for hot work, had just commenced
when it ended."

The one-sided statements above alluded to in-
duced Mr. Frederick Milnes Edge, an English gen-

tleman of high character, to prepare a complete story of the engagement, from which the following is condensed :

"The importance of the engagement between the United States sloop-of-war Kearsarge, and the Confederate privateer Alabama, cannot be estimated by the size of the two vessels. The conflict off Cherbourg on Sunday, the 19th of June, was the first decisive engagement between shipping propelled by steam, and the first test of the merits of modern naval artillery. It was, moreover, a contest for superiority between the ordnance of Europe and America, whilst the result furnishes us with *data* wherefrom to estimate the relative advantages of rifled and smooth-bore cannon at short range.

"Perhaps no greater or more numerous misrepresentations were ever made in regard to an engagement than in reference to the one in question. The first news of the conflict came to us enveloped in a mass of statemnts, the greater part of which, not to use an unparliamentary expression, was diametrically opposed to the truth.

"Within a few days of the fight, the writer of these pages crossed from London to Cherbourg for the purpose of obtaining, by personal examination, full and precise information in reference to the engagement. It would seem as though misrepresentation, if not positive falsehood, were inseparable from everything connected with the Alabama, for on reaching the French naval station he was positively assured by the people on shore that nobody was permitted to board the Kearsarge. Preferring, however, to substantiate the truth of these allega-

tions from the officers of the vessel themselves, he
sailed out to the sloop, receiving on his arrival
an immediate and polite reception from Captain
Winslow and his gallant subordinates. During
the six days he remained at Cherbourg, he found
the Kearsarge open to the inspection, above and
below, of anybody who chose to visit her ; and he
frequently heard surprise expressed by English and
French visitors that representations on shore were
so inconsonant with the truth of the case.

"I found the Kearsarge lying under the guns of
the French ship-of-the-line 'Napoleon,' two cables'
length from that vessel, and about a mile and
a half from the harbor ; she had not moved from
that anchorage since entering the port of Cherbourg, and no repairs whatever had been effected
in her hull since the fight. I had thus full opportunity to examine the extent of her damage, and
she certainly did not look at all like a vessel which
had just been engaged in one of the hottest con-
flicts of modern times.

"The Kearsarge, in size, is by no means the terri-
ble craft represented by those who, for some reason
or other, seek to detract from the honor of her victory ; she appeared to me a mere yacht in compar-
ison with the shipping around her, and disappoint-
ed many of the visitors who came to see her. The
relative proportions of the antagonists were as follows :

	Alabama.	*Kearsarge.*
Length over all,	220 ft.	232 ft.
Length of keel,	210 ft.	198½ ft.
Beam,	32 ft.	33 ft.
Depth,	17 ft.	16½ ft.
Horse power, 2 engines of 300 each		400 h. p.
Tonnage,	1,040	1,031

" The Alabama was a barque-rigged screw propeller, and the heaviness of her rig, and, above all, the greater size and height of her masts, would give her the appearance of a much larger vessel than her antagonist. The masts of the latter are disproportionately low and small; she has never carried more than top-sail yards, and depends for her speed upon her machinery alone. It is to be questioned whether the Alabama, with all her reputation for velocity, could, in her best trim, outsteam her rival. The log-book of the Kearsarge, which I was courteously permitted to examine, frequently shows a speed of upwards of fourteen knots the hour, and her engineers state that her machinery was never in better working order than at present. I have not seen engines more compact in form, nor, apparently, in finer condition, looking in every part as though they were fresh from the workshop, instead of being, as they are, half through the third year of the cruise.

" The armaments of the Alabama and Kearsarge were as follows:

ARMAMENT OF THE ALABAMA.

One 7-inch Blakely rifle.
One 8-inch smooth-bore (68-pounder).
Six 32-pounders.

ARMAMENT OF THE KEARSARGE.

Two 11-inch smooth-bore guns.
One 30-pounder rifle.
Four 32-pounders.

" It will therefore be seen that the Alabama had the advantage of the Kearsarge,—at all events in the number of her guns; whilst the weight of the latter's broadside was only some 20 per cent. greater than her own. This disparity, however, was more than made up by the greater rapidity of the Alabama's firing. Each vessel fought with all her guns, with the exception in either case of one 32-pounder on the starboard side; but the struggle was really decided by the two 11-inch Dahlgren smooth-bores of the Kearsarge against the 7-inch Blakely rifle and the heavy 68-pounder pivot of the Alabama.

"The Kearsarge lay off Fayal towards the latter part of April, 1863, on the look-out for a notorious blockade-runner named the 'Juno.' Being short of coal, which made her sit high out of water, and, fearing some attempts at opposition on the part of her prey, the first officer of the sloop, Lieutenant-Commander James S. Thornton, suggested to Captain Winslow the advisability of hanging her two sheet-anchor cables over her sides, so as to protect her midship section. Mr. Thornton had served on board the flag-ship of Admiral Farragut, the 'Hartford,' when she and the rest of the Federal fleet ran the forts of the Mississippi to reach New Orleans; and he made the suggestion at Fayal through having seen the advantage gained by it on that occasion. I copy the following extract from the log-book of the Kearsarge:

"'HORTA BAY, FAYAL (May 1st, 1863).

"'From 8 to Merid. Wind E. N. E. (F 2). Weather b. c. Strapped, loaded, and fused (5 sec. fuse) 13 XI-inch shell. Commenced armor plating ship, using sheet chain. Weighed kedge anchor.

(Signed)

"'E. M. STODDARD, *Acting Master*.'

" This operation of chain-armoring took three days, and was effected without assistance from the shore, and at an expense of material of seventy-five dollars (£15). In order to make the addition less unsightly, the chains were boxed over with ¾-inch deal boards, forming a case, or box, which stood out at right angles from the vessel's sides. This box would naturally excite curiosity in every port where the Kearsarge touched, and no mystery was made as to what the boarding covered. Capt. Semmes was perfectly cognizant of the entire affair, for he spoke about it to his officers and crew several days prior to the 19th of June, declaring that the chains were only attached together with rope-yarns, and would drop into the water when struck with the first shot. I was so informed by his wounded men lying in the naval hospital at Cherbourg. Whatever might be the value for defence of this chain-plating, it was only struck once during the engagement, so far as I could discover by a long and close inspection. Some of the officers of the Kearsarge asserted to me that it was struck twice, whilst others deny that declaration : in one spot, however, a 32-pounder shot broke in the deal covering and smashed a single link, two thirds of which fell into the water. The remainder is in my possession, and proves to be of the ordinary 5¼-inch chain. Had the cable been struck by the rifled 120-pounder instead of by a 32, the result might have been different ; but in any case the damage would have amounted to nothing serious, for the vessel's side was hit five feet above the water-line, and nowhere in the vicinity of the boilers or machinery. Capt. Semmes evidently regarded this protection of the chains as little worth, for he might have adopted

the same plan before engaging the Kearsarge ; but
he confined himself to taking on board 150 tons of
coal *as a protection to his boilers*, which, in addition to the 200 tons already in his bunkers, would
bring him pretty low in the water. The Kearsarge, on the contrary, was deficient in her coal,
and she took what was necessary on board during
my stay at Cherbourg.

"On the morning of the battle an excursion train
arrived from Paris, and visitors were received at
the terminus of the railway by the boatmen of the
port, who offered them boats for the purpose of
seeing *a genuine naval battle which was to take
place during the day*. Turning such a memorable
occurrence to practical uses, Mons. Rondin, a celebrated photographic artist on the *Place d'Armes*
at Cherbourg, prepared the necessary chemicals,
plates, and *camera*, and placed himself on the
summit of the old church tower in happy juxta-
position with his establishment. I was only able
to see the negative, but that was sufficient to show
that the artist had obtained a very fine view of the
exciting contest. Five days, however, had elapsed
since Captain Semmes sent his challenge to Captain Winslow through the Confederate agent, Mon-
sieur Bonfils,—surely time sufficient for him to
make all the preparations which he considered
necessary. Meanwhile the Kearsarge was cruising
to and fro at sea, outside the breakwater.

"So soon as the Alabama was made out, the
Kearsarge immediately headed seaward and steamed off the coast, the object being to get a sufficient
distance from the land to obviate any possible in-
fringement of French jurisdiction ; and, secondly,
in case of the battle going against the Alabama,

the latter could not retreat into port. When this was accomplished, the Kearsarge was turned shortly round and steered immediately for the Alabama, Captain Winslow desiring to get within close range, as his guns were shotted with five-seconds shell. The interval between the two vessels being reduced to a mile, or thereabouts, the Alabama sheered and discharged a broadside, nearly a raking fire, at the Kearsarge. More speed was given to the latter to shorten the distance, and a slight sheer to prevent raking. The Alabama fired a second broadside, and part of a third, while her antagonist was closing; and, at the expiration of ten or twelve minutes from the Alabama's opening shot, the Kearsarge discharged her first broadside. The action henceforward continued in a circle, the distance between the two vessels being about seven hundred yards; this, at all events, is the opinion of the Federal commander and his officers, for their guns were sighted at that range, and their shell burst in and over the privateer. The speed of the two vessels during the engagement did not exceed eight knots the hour.

"At the expiration of one hour and two minutes from the first gun, the Alabama hauled down her colors and fired a lee gun (according to the statements of her officers), in token of surrender. Captain Winslow could not, however, believe that the enemy had struck, as his own vessel had received so little damage; and it was only when a boat came off from the Alabama that her true condition was known. The 11-inch shell from the Kearsarge, thrown with fifteen pounds of powder at seven hundred yards' range, had gone clean through the starboard side of the privateer, bursting in the port side and tearing great gaps in her timber and planking. This was plainly obvious when the Alabama settled by the stern and raised the forepart of her hull high out of water.

"The Kearsarge was struck twenty-seven times during the conflict, and fired in all one hundred and seventy-three (173) shots. The trifling damage received by the Kearsarge proves the exceedingly bad fire of the Alabama, notwithstanding the numbers of men on board the latter belonging to our 'Naval Reserve,' and the trained hands from the gunnery ship 'Excellent.' I was informed by some of the paroled prisoners on shore at Cherbourg that Captain Semmes fired rapidly at the commencement of the action ' in order to frighten the Yankees,' nearly all the officers and crew being, as he was well aware, volunteers from the merchant service. At the expiration of twenty minutes after the Kearsarge discharged the first broadside, continuing the battle in a leisurely, cool manner, Semmes remarked,—'Confound them ! they've been fighting twenty minutes, and they're as cool as posts.' The probabilities are, that the crew of the Federal vessel had learnt not to regard as dangerous the rapid and hap-hazard practice of the Alabama.

"From the time of her first reaching Cherbourg until she finally quitted the port, the Kearsarge never received the slightest assistance from shore, with the exception of that rendered by a boiler-maker in patching up her funnel. Every other repair was completed by her own hands, and she might have crossed the Atlantic immediately after the action without difficulty.

"Such are the facts relating to the memorable

action off Cherbourg on the 19th of June, 1864. The Alabama went down riddled through and through with shot; and, as she sank beneath the green waves of the Channel, not a single cheer arose from the victors. The order was given, and in perfect silence this terror of American commerce plunged to her last resting-place.

"There is but one key to the victory. The two vessels were, as nearly as possible, equals in size, speed, armament, and crew, and the contest was decided by the superiority of the 11-inch Dahlgren guns of the Kearsarge over the Blakely rifle and the vaunted 68-pounder of the Alabama, in conjunction with the greater coolness and surer aim of the former's crew. The Kearsarge was not, as represented, specially armed and manned for destroying her foe, but is in every respect similar to all the vessels of her class (third-rate) in the United States Navy.

"It appears that out of one hundred and sixty-three officers and crew of the sloop-of-war Kearsarge, there are only eleven persons foreign born. The men of the Alabama, almost without exception, are subjects of Her Majesty the Queen."

William Smith, a quartermaster of the Kearsarge, was captain of one of the eleven-inch guns, which did such execution that Semmes offered his men a reward to silence it. One shell, which was believed to have been fired from Smith's gun, killed and wounded eighteen men in the Alabama, and disabled a cannon.

The thunder of the battle was heard across the

channel in churches on the south coast of England.

Capt. Winslow was publicly thanked by the Navy Department " for the ability displayed in this combat," was advanced to the grade of commodore, received the thanks of congress, and an extension of ten years on the active list of the navy. Because of the renown which this affair gave him in Europe, he was, in 1866, on the recommendation of Secretary Seward, given command of the Gulf Squadron, while the question of the withdrawal of the French army from Mexico was pending. He reached the grade of admiral in July, 1870.

Lieut. Commander Thornton was advanced ten numbers on the naval register, and ultimately reached the rank of captain. He died in Philadelphia, May 14, 1875, in consequence of injuries received at sea while in command of a naval vessel in the South Pacific ocean.

It will be observed, by reference to various dates in this collection, that Mr. Fox's claim as to the naming of the Kearsarge was not broached until after the death of both Admiral Winslow and Capt. Thornton, but immediately thereafter.

Secretary Welles, in his letter of Sept. 27, 1875, which has been referred to in the foregoing pages, makes the suggestion that the honor to which the true Kearsarge is entitled should be waived as " an award to the fair and the brave." The time may

come when it will be in order to consider that
suggestion. It will be, if ever, when persons edu-
cated at their country's expense, found doing bu-
reau duty in time of war, tying and untying red
tape, and higgling with contractors, are deemed
fairer and braver than the men who fought and
sunk the Alabama.

www.ingramcontent.com/pod-product-compliance
Lightning Source LLC
Chambersburg PA
CBHW021236260626
47172CB00002B/791